Flashing
FIRE ENGINES

For Renée, Eric, Cornelia and Saskia – T.M.

*The Publisher thanks London Fire Brigade Headquarters and
the New York City Fire Department Public Information Office
for their kind assistance in the development of this book.*

KINGFISHER
An imprint of Kingfisher Publications Plc
New Penderel House, 283-288 High Holborn, London WC1V 7HZ

First published in hardback by Kingfisher 1998

1RD+AURA/0502/TWP/RPR(FR)/150ENSOMA

Text copyright © Tony Mitton 1998
Illustrations copyright © Ant Parker 1998

A CIP catalogue record for this book is available from the British Library.

ISBN 0 7534 0196 7

Printed in Singapore

Flashing
FIRE ENGINES

Tony Mitton
and
Ant Parker

KINGFISHER

Big, bold fire engines, waiting day and night,

ready for a rescue or a blazing fire to fight.

As soon as there's a fire alarm,
the engine starts to roar.

The firefighters jump aboard –
it rumbles out the door.

Watch the engine speeding, on its daring dash.

Hear its siren screaming. See its bright lights flash.

the crew are dressed and ready
as the engine zooms along

When the engine finds the fire,
it quickly pulls up near.

The crew jump out, unroll the hose
and get out all the gear.

The hose has got a nozzle
that shoots a jet of spray.
It squirts right at the blazing flames
and sizzles them away.

The water tank is empty soon,
so where can more be found?
The engine's pump can pull it up
from pipes below the ground.

The fire is hot and roaring.
It makes a lot of smoke.

The firefighters put on masks,
otherwise they'd choke.

The ladder rises upward. It reaches for the sky.
A fire engine's ladder stretches up so very high!

Sometimes there's a platform, right up at the top.
It waits beside the window. Then into it you hop.

At last the fire's extinguished.
The flames are all put out.

plop!

plop!

Lower the ladder. Roll the hose.
"Hooray!" the fire crew shout.

Back inside the station,
the crew can take a break.

But the fire engine's ready
and it's waiting wide-awake.

Fire Engine bits

helmet

this is a hard hat that protects the firefighter's head

fireproof coats and trousers

these are made from special material that does not burn easily and protects firefighters from the fire

masks and tanks

we cannot breathe in smoky air so firefighters carry clean air in **tanks** on their backs and this flows into their **masks**

siren

this makes a loud noise to tell people to move out of the way and let the fire engine pass

pump

this sucks water from the tank and pushes it out through tubes called **hoses** – it also gets water from underground through big taps in the street called **hydrants**

water tank

this is inside the middle of the fire engine and holds water to fight the fire – some fire engines carry foam, too

hose connects to pump